This book belongs to

_____

THE MISSING SHAPES MIX-UP

Published by Advance Publishers
Winter Park, Florida

© 1997 Disney Enterprises, Inc.
All rights reserved. Printed in the United States.
No part of this book may be reproduced or copied in any form
without written permission from the copyright owner.

Written by Wendy Wax   Edited by Bonnie Brook
Penciled by Jeff Shelly   Painted by Brad McMahon
Designed by Design Five
Cover art by Peter Emslie
Cover design by Irene Yap

ISBN: 1-885222-79-3
10 9 8 7 6 5 4 3 2 1

One morning, Mickey gave Minnie a red vase.

"Oh, Mickey!" she said. "It's shaped like a heart!"

But just as Minnie went to put down the vase, Mickey's nephews, Morty and Ferdie, raced by on their way outside to play. They bumped into Minnie, and she dropped the vase, breaking it in two.

"We're sorry," said Morty.

"Don't worry, Minnie," said Mickey. "The boys will fix the vase for you."

"May we do it outside?" asked Ferdie.

"Well, okay," said Mickey, "but no playing until the vase is fixed."

As the boys went outside, Mickey and Minnie went into the kitchen for a snack of fresh fruit—peaches, plums, and oranges.

"They're all round," said Mickey, laughing.

"That's because my favorite shape is the circle," said Minnie. "I like beads, buttons, and coins, too."

Just then, Morty and Ferdie came back inside.

"Did you fix the vase?" asked Mickey.

"We're just letting the glue dry," said Morty.

"Do you have any games we can play while we wait, Aunt Minnie?" asked Ferdie.

"I'm afraid not," said Minnie.

"Gosh, look at all those circles," said Ferdie.

Minnie had laid all her beads, buttons, and coins on the table.

"I have an idea for a game," said Mickey. "Do you have some paper and scissors, Minnie?"

A little while later, Mickey, Minnie, Morty, and Ferdie were all seated at the table.

"First, we'll cut out shapes," said Mickey. "Then we'll glue them together to make pictures."

Mickey cut out a bunch of squares.

Minnie cut some circles.

Morty made triangles.

Ferdie made rectangles.

Minnie showed Morty how to draw an oval.
"It looks like a long circle," said Morty.

Mickey showed Ferdie how to make
a square out of two triangles.

A little while later, the table was covered with squares, circles, triangles, rectangles, ovals, and even diamonds and stars.

"Now pick out some shapes, and see if you can make pictures," said Mickey.

Minnie made a purple flower.

Morty made a picture of a sailboat.

Mickey made a bear wearing a bow tie.

Ferdie placed a triangle on top of a rectangle to make a circus tent.

"Wow! You can make almost anything out of these shapes," said Morty.

"Maybe we should go check on the vase now," said Ferdie.

"Thanks for the game," said the boys as they ran outside.

"Gawrsh, look at all those shapes," said Goofy. He was standing in Minnie's window. "I collect squares. Do you want to see them?"

"Sure," said Mickey.

Mickey and Minnie followed Goofy to his house.

There was a square sandbox in Goofy's front yard.

Inside his house, Goofy showed Mickey and Minnie some boxes.

"There are six sides to every box," said Mickey. "That means you can collect six squares per box."

Goofy tried to count the sides of a box, but he got confused.

"We need to get back to Morty and Ferdie," said Mickey.

"Thanks for showing us your squares, Goofy," said Minnie.

Back at Minnie's kitchen, Mickey and Minnie noticed that there wasn't a button, bead, or coin in sight.

On the table was a note. Minnie read it aloud:

Dear Aunt Minnie: We borrowed some of your circles. We'll bring them back later. Thanks. Love, Morty and Ferdie.

"Gosh," said Minnie. "I wonder why they wanted all those circles." Just then the telephone rang.

It was Goofy calling to talk to Mickey.

"I wanted to tell you that Morty and Ferdie were just here, in case you were looking for them," said Goofy. "They borrowed some of my boxes."

"Thanks," said Mickey as he hung up.

"I don't know what those boys are up to," he said, "but I think it's time to find out."

"Maybe we should split up," said Minnie. "I'll go check with Donald."

"And I'll call Goofy back to see if he can help," said Mickey.

Minnie went to see Donald.

"Hi, Minnie," said Donald. "I just saw Morty and Ferdie. They borrowed some playing cards for a project. They said they needed rectangles."

"I wonder why," said Minnie, taking notes.

Goofy noticed Clarabelle Cow walking down the street.

"Have you seen Morty and Ferdie, Clarabelle?" asked Goofy.

"Yes, I just saw them," she said. "They borrowed all of my chickens' eggs."

"Gawrsh," said Goofy. "Ovals."

Mickey knocked on Daisy's front door.

"Did Morty and Ferdie stop by to borrow any shapes?" he asked.

"Yes," Daisy said. "My kite."

Mickey read over his notes. "A kite, hmmm . . . shaped like a diamond."

"Hey, Goofy," Horace Horsecollar called. "Something strange is going on. Morty and Ferdie said they needed to borrow my brass triangle."

"Gee," said Goofy. "You mean the one you play in the band?"

"That's right," said Horace.

Finally, Mickey, Minnie, and Goofy got back together and compared notes.

"Morty and Ferdie have borrowed all the shapes in town," said Minnie.

"Not *all* of them," said Mickey. "That would mean everything was missing, since everything in the world has a shape."

"Gawrsh, even I do," said Goofy, looking at his shadow on the sidewalk.

Just then Grandma Duck walked up.

"I just baked star-shaped cookies," she said. "Morty and Ferdie asked if they could borrow them."

"Gosh, stars, too!" cried Mickey.

Suddenly they heard the beating of a drum. *Boom, boom, boom!*

"What's that noise?" said Mickey.

Ding. Ding. Ding. Now, they heard other sounds.

"That sounds like Horace's brass triangle," said Minnie.

They followed the sound to Mickey's backyard—and couldn't believe their eyes.

"A circus!" cried Minnie.

"Made up of shapes!" Mickey said.

Morty was dressed as the ringmaster and was flying Daisy's kite, with Donald's playing cards dangling on the string. Ferdie was dressed as a clown in a jumpsuit decorated with Minnie's buttons and beads.

"We made this circus for Minnie to show her how sorry we were for breaking her vase," said Morty.

"Why didn't you tell us?" asked Mickey.

"We wanted it to be a surprise," Ferdie answered.

Soon everybody arrived to
see how their shapes helped
make the circus. They watched
Morty juggle the eggs. They
ate Grandma Duck's star-
shaped cookies. They cheered
as Pluto jumped through
a hoop held by Ferdie.

"And now for the contest," said Morty.

"Minnie, we need you to volunteer," said Ferdie. "If you choose the right box, you'll win a prize."

Minnie chose a box, took off the lid, and—

"My vase!" Minnie cried. "It's fixed!"

When the circus was over, Morty and Ferdie returned all the shapes to their owners.

"Uncle Mickey," said Morty, "may we borrow one last thing?"

"Sure," said Mickey.

A few minutes later, Morty and Ferdie handed Minnie some freshly cut roses from Mickey's garden.

"Oh, thank you!" said Minnie, placing the flowers in her heart-shaped vase. "Maybe the heart is my favorite shape, after all."

"I couldn't agree more," said Mickey.